Esther's Story

Diane Wolkstein

Illustrated by Juan Wijngaard

Morrow Junior Books   New York

Pronunciation Guide

Adar   ah-DAR

Ahasuerus   a-ha-SWER-us

Hadassah   ha-DAS-ah

Haman   HAY-men

Hegai   HEH-guy

Mitra   MEE-trah

Mordecai   MOR-de-ky

Purim   POOR-um

Shirin   shih-REEN

shofar   show-FAR

Susa   SOO-sah

Vashti   VASH-tee

Author's Note

Esther's Story is woven together from the biblical Book of Esther, oral legends, and my own musings. I culled many of the oral legends from Rabbi Yaakov Culi's book on Esther, *Yalkut Me'am Lo'ez*. Other legends were told to me by my rabbi, Shlomo Carlebach. My thanks to Rabbi Carlebach, Andrea Curley, Professor Tamara Green of Hunter College, Professor Ed Greenstein of the Jewish Theological Seminary, Judith Kroll, and Susan Thomas for their suggestions and careful readings of the manuscript.

Gouache on paper was used for the full-color illustrations. The text type is 14.5-point Goudy Old Style BT.

Text copyright © 1996 by Diane Wolkstein
Illustrations copyright © 1996 by Juan Wijngaard

Printed in Hong Kong by South China Printing Company (1988) Ltd.
1 2 3 4 5 6 7 8 9 10

Library of Congress Cataloging-in-Publication Data
Wolkstein, Diane.   Esther's story/Diane Wolkstein; illustrated by Juan Wijngaard.   p. cm.
ISBN 0-688-12127-6 (trade)—ISBN 0-688-12128-4 (library)
1. Esther, Queen of Persia—Juvenile literature.   2. Bible. O.T.—Biography—Juvenile literature.
3. Bible stories, English—O.T. Esther.   [1. Esther, Queen of Persia.   2. Bible stories—O.T.]
I. Wijngaard, Juan, ill.   II. Title.   BS580.E8W65   1995   222'.909505—dc20   94-15473   CIP   AC

For Deena Metzger and Lorna Roberts,
women of beauty and courage
D. W.

For Erin
J. W.

My uncle went to the king's banquet. But he did not eat the food. That's because we are Jewish and eat food prepared in a different way from the Persians'. Uncle Mordecai said that the guests lay on silver couches in the courtyard garden and were served whatever they chose to drink in gold goblets. The smell of the blossoming trees perfumed the air, and the colored stones on the floor formed patterns in the shape of roses. How I wish I had been there.

The banquet goes on for seven nights. Since Uncle is one of the king's judges, he has been invited all seven nights. King Ahasuerus is giving the banquet to celebrate the completion of his great throne, which has taken three years to build.

Before leaving for the banquet, Uncle Mordecai gave me this diary. He has taken care of me ever since I can remember. My mother and father died many years ago. Even though I am eleven and am too young to go with him, Uncle says I can still write about what is happening.

I woke up when Uncle came home. From the way he opened the door, I could tell he was troubled. But when he saw me, he smiled and said, "Here you are, Hadassah, and just at the moment when I am thinking of you. How strange are the workings of heaven and earth."

Uncle Mordecai took me on his lap and said, "Your mother named you Hadassah for the sweet-smelling myrtle. But tonight I shall give you the new name of Esther, which means secret or concealed. Listen, my child, to what happened at the banquet, and remember that although our lives may change, our god is constant.

"Tonight Queen Vashti, the queen of all Persia, refused to go to the king when he called for her, so she has been banished. Tomorrow a search for a new queen begins throughout the one hundred and twenty-seven lands of Persia."

"Will the new queen be beautiful?" I asked.

"As beautiful as you are."

"Will she be kind?"

"As kind as you are."

"And brave?"

"As brave as you are. Can you remember that your new name is Esther?"

"Of course." I had more questions. But Uncle kissed me good night, and somehow I knew that the answers, even if I asked for them, were not yet known.

It is not so easy to have a new name. Half the time when Uncle calls me I forget he means me, so I don't answer. Hadassah belongs to my grandmother, who lived in Jerusalem.

Esther, my new name, is Jewish and Persian, like me. In Persian Esther is the goddess Ishtar, who is the goddess of love and war. She is also the first planet to appear every night in the sky. I often watch for her in the evening. I think it is very brave of her to appear all alone when it is dark.

At twelve I know for certain I am Esther. Persian tutors teach me to sew and cook, to sing and dance and recite poems.

With my sewing teacher, I'm working on a beautiful dress that has all the colors I love: red and pink and purple, with a little blue and green.

Everything has changed!

I am no longer at home. Two days ago, a friend of Uncle Mordecai who is also a judge at the King's Gate came for dinner. I wore my new dress, and when he saw me, he threw out his arms and said, "A queen, you look like a queen!" We laughed. But the next day, a guard arrived and brought me to the palace.

The girls here are from many countries. They tell me that we have been chosen so that the king can decide which one of us he wants for his queen. They are all much more beautiful than I am. I don't want to be queen. I miss Uncle Mordecai. I want to go home.

Three months have gone by and I am slowly getting used to life in the palace. I have made friends with many of the girls. Hegai, who looks after us, goes to the market each week and brings us back dresses and jewelry and perfume. The days pass quickly, but at night, some of the girls cry from homesickness. Last night I held Shirin's hand and sang to her until she fell asleep. I am fortunate that Uncle Mordecai can visit me.

Last time Uncle was here, he brought my favorite food and told me stories of our ancestors. When I asked him what protected Abraham and Sarah when they traveled to foreign lands, he said that Sarah was not only beautiful but she had secret powers that even Abraham did not understand.

Uncle reminded me of the promise I had made the night he gave me my new name. I am not to tell anyone that I am Jewish. I don't know why he worries so much about this. The king allows everyone in the kingdom to worship which-ever gods they wish. I don't want to grow up being afraid because I'm Jewish.

It happened so quickly I hardly had time to prepare. Yesterday morning, after four years, Hegai came to me and said the king wished to see me that evening.

I bathed and Hegai gave me the king's favorite perfume. I wore my red dress, the one embroidered with stars and flowers. Hegai's assistant wove tiny pink roses into my braids. I was led through seven gates into the part of the palace where the king lives. No one is ever allowed to walk through the seven gates without permission and an escort. I was eager to see this king who had been searching for a wife for so many years.

The king was standing by the window. He looked a little lonely. His arms were folded. I folded mine in the same way. He scratched his head. I scratched mine, and a tiny pink rose fell to the floor. As I bent down to pick it up, the king said, "How beautiful you are!"

I put the rose in his curly hair and said, "How beautiful *you* are!"

He laughed. I liked his laugh. It was deep and growly and unexpected.

"Laugh again!" I said, and I tickled him.

A big happy laugh came bursting out of him, like water from a fountain.

When he stopped laughing, he picked up the crown from the table and, without asking my name, said, "You, my shining one, shall be queen."

Some days when I look in the mirror, I see the queen of Persia. Other days I see Esther, who was once Hadassah. I have my own rooms and seven servants. I like them all, especially Mitra. She has the kindest heart of anyone I've ever seen. If someone is sad or has troubles, she is the first to help.

To celebrate my becoming queen, the king gave many banquets. We had wonderful food, and I ate as much as the king. The king often asks me about my relatives, but each time I have found an answer that is not an answer. We eat a lot, we laugh a lot, and everyone in the palace is happy.

No, everyone is not happy. There is trouble now. Uncle Mordecai told me that at the King's Gate he overheard two relatives of Queen Vashti whispering together in a strange language. They were plotting to poison the king for sending Vashti away. Uncle, who knows seventy languages, understood them and said I was to tell the king as soon as possible. The king was busy choosing a new prime minister, but as soon as I told him, the plotters were caught and killed, and Uncle Mordecai's brave deed was written down in the *Book of Records* in front of the king.

The new prime minister's name is Haman. He speaks harshly to everyone and rarely smiles. Uncle Mordecai distrusts Haman and refuses to bow to him, which makes Haman very angry. Sometimes I wish that Uncle Mordecai was not so stubborn.

Yesterday when Haman walked out through the King's Gate, Uncle again refused to bow to him and Haman became furious. My servant Mitra, who is friendly with Haman's servant, told me that Haman spoke to the other judges. When he found out that Uncle Mordecai is a Jew, he decided he would kill all the Jews.

I can hardly believe the horrifying news that Mitra has just told me. She said that last night Haman threw dice to find out which would be the best day to destroy the Jews. He and his sons took turns and threw the dice until Haman had his answer. My heart is pounding with fear. I have sent word to Uncle Mordecai to come to the palace at once.

Uncle Mordecai is wandering through the streets of the city in sackcloth, weeping bitterly. Even though I sent Mitra with proper clothes for Uncle so that he could enter the palace, he refuses. Instead, he gave Mitra a copy of a notice that Haman has sent throughout the kingdom. The notice is engraved with the king's stamp and states that on the thirteenth day of Adar, the month before spring begins, all Jews—young and old—are to be killed and their property seized. Uncle Mordecai also enclosed a note to me, saying:

Haman offered the king a great sum of money—ten thousand silver talents—for the right to do what he wishes with the Jews. I cannot sit as judge anymore. How can I, if my people are to be killed? My dearest Esther, you must go to the king, reveal who you are, and beg for his help.

I wrote back and told Uncle Mordecai that, as he well knows, no one may see the king without permission. The king has not sent for me for thirty days. If I force my way and am killed, what use will I be? But then Uncle Mordecai sent a second note, saying:

Long ago, I was told by a holy woman from Jerusalem that you would be queen of Persia. This seemed impossible. But when Vashti was banished, I saw that what I thought impossible might be coming about for a purpose. My dear Esther, it may be that you have become queen to save your people. Although you are loved, do not think you are safe. Already, outside Susa, in the other lands of the kingdom, they have begun to kill our people.

I am afraid.

In this great palace with its guards and cooks, its messengers and hundreds of servants, there is no one I can turn to. Not even Mitra.

I sit at the window and watch the sky grow dark. As the light of the first star appears in the heavens, the words of Isaiah suddenly come to me: *When your hair is white, I will be with you. I made you. I will care for you. I will sustain and rescue you.*

There *is* someone for me to turn to.

I have sent word to Uncle Mordecai, asking that he and the Jews of Susa fast and pray for me. In three days I will go to the king. If I am killed, then I will be killed.

For the past three days I have not eaten. I have read and wept and prayed. Then today, as I was lying on the floor of my room, I heard a gigantic cry—it seemed to rise up from the bottom of the earth, loud enough to pierce the heavens. It was the sound of thousands of rams' horns! Uncle Mordecai must have had each of the priests in the city blow his shofar to give me strength.

I bathed. As Mitra helped me to prepare myself, I thought of Sarah and prayed that her beauty and power would be with me. I put on my crown and the dress the king likes best.

I started toward the throne room. The guards did not stop me. I walked through the first, the second, and the third gates. At the fourth gate, my legs began to tremble. I walked more slowly. I passed through the fifth and sixth gates. As I came to the seventh gate, I wondered if these were my last minutes to live. Then I heard the sound of the shofar, and I pushed the last gate open.

The king was sitting on his golden throne, dressed in royal purple robes. For a moment, I did not breathe. Then the king turned and, seeing me, lowered his gold scepter, the sign that I am allowed to speak.

"My dear wife, what is your wish?"

I touched the scepter and said, "My wish, Your Majesty, if it pleases you, is that you and Haman attend a banquet in my room tonight."

Haman was beaming when he arrived this evening at the banquet. After the king and Haman drank and ate, the king again asked me, "My dear wife, what is your wish?"

Again I answered, "O my king, if I have pleased you, my wish is that you and Haman come tomorrow evening for another banquet in my room. Then I will reveal what you wish to know."

I do not know how much longer I can delay answering the king. I am waiting for a sign.

Not long after I fell asleep, the sound of hammering woke me up. I went to the window and by the light of the torches saw Haman and his sons building a great gallows across from the palace. Who does Haman intend to hang on the gallows? I hope Uncle Mordecai is safe.

I cannot sleep. There are footsteps in the hall. The king also cannot sleep and has sent for the *Book of Records*. His servant sometimes reads it to him at night. It is so boring, it usually puts him to sleep immediately.

What a day! Today is surely the day of all days! I woke early this morning. The hammering had stopped, and in its place I heard drums and shouts of laughter. I went out onto the balcony and saw the most amazing sight.

A royal parade with two thousand buglers, five thousand drummers, and ten thousand soldiers was passing by. And who was at the head of the parade? Who?

Uncle! Uncle Mordecai rode on the king's white horse, dressed in the king's purple robes! And who led Uncle Mordecai's horse? *Haman,* whose face was red with shame!

I shouted with surprise and ran to find Mitra. Last night, she told me, when the king was listening to the *Book of Records,* he realized he had never rewarded Mordecai for saving his life. So this morning at dawn he summoned his prime minister and asked, "How shall the king reward a man he wishes to honor?"

Haman, certain that the king was speaking of him, replied, "Let the king hold a great parade. And let the noblest prince in the kingdom dress the man of honor in His Majesty's clothes and lead him through the streets on His Majesty's white horse, crying, 'This is how the king honors a great man!'"

I am so happy. I want to congratulate Uncle, but there is no time. I must prepare for the banquet.

It is done!

Last night while the king and Haman were drinking, the king asked me, "Now, my dear wife, tell me, what is your wish? Even if it is half the kingdom, it will be yours."

I answered in one breath, for I did not dare to stop until I had finished. "Your Majesty, my wish is for my life and for the lives of my people. I would not ask you this if we had been sold to be slaves, but we have been sold to be slaughtered on the thirteenth day of Adar."

"Who has issued such an order?" the king asked.

I pointed to Haman with tears of anger. "That man. That evil man used your signet ring to sign a decree ordering that all Jews be killed. Since I am a Jew, I too will die."

Trembling with anger, the king stood up. He stumbled out of the room into the garden. Haman rushed to the couch on which I was lying and pleaded, "Your Majesty, I beg you. Spare my life—"

Just then the king returned, and Haman, in terror, tripped and fell on top of me. As I cried out, the king shouted in fury, "Does this man dare attack the queen when I am in the room?"

No words came out of Haman's mouth. The guards seized him, and one of them said, "Your Majesty, the gallows that Haman built are empty!"

"Then let Haman die," the king cried. "Let him die on his own gallows!"

On the day of Haman's death, the king gave me Haman's house and wealth, and made Uncle Mordecai prime minister. I was afraid to ask for anything more, but the decree ordering the destruction of my people had not been changed, and each day they were being killed. I had to go to the king. I could not wait. As the king was about to call for his musicians, I fell on the floor before him and wept. The king lowered his gold scepter, allowing me to speak.

I stood up and pleaded from the center of my heart. "Your Majesty, if I have pleased you, I beg you to stop the decree ordering the death of my people. I cannot go on living if my people are destroyed."

"My dear wife," the king said, "once an order has gone out sealed with the king's signet ring, it cannot be changed. That is the law."

I looked at the king. I did not speak. But I did not take my eyes from his.

At last the king shook his head and said, "But—a new decree can be issued! What the new prime minister writes can also be sealed with the king's signet ring." The king summoned Uncle Mordecai and handed him his ring.

Uncle sent at once for the king's scribes, who wrote letters in one hundred and twenty-seven languages stating that on the thirteenth day of Adar, Jews may defend themselves against anyone who attacks them. The letters were sealed with the king's signet ring and were rushed to the one hundred and twenty-seven countries of the kingdom on the fastest horses.

For many months Mordecai and I have lived in fear. Two days ago, although all the governors and many of the people knew that it was not the king's wish, Haman's supporters attacked the Jews. Outside the capital, on the thirteenth day of Adar, our people joined together and in a single day defeated all those who attacked them.

But here in Susa the fighting, led by Haman's sons, was fierce. At the end of the day, the king spoke to me, saying, "The Jews have killed five hundred men as well as ten of Haman's sons. My dearest wife, what is your wish?"

"If it pleases Your Majesty, allow the Jews in Susa one more day to defend themselves against Haman's supporters."

The king agreed, and, the next day, the Jews in the capital defeated those who attacked them, and the fighting ended.

Yesterday, the Jews in the other lands celebrated their victory. Today, we are celebrating in Susa. Our hearts are full. We run here and there, laughing and making jokes. Everywhere there are banquets. We eat and drink and hug each other. We dance with great joy and relief.

Mordecai has sent letters to the Jews in all the lands, urging them to remember the miracle in which they played a part. Because of Mordecai's letters and what the Jews had seen, in every community and every land, they have agreed to make the fourteenth and fifteenth days of Adar a holiday. They are calling the holiday Purim after the Persian word *pur*, which means dice or fate. Haman tried to destroy the Jews. Instead, he destroyed himself.

I, also, am writing to my people. I want to thank them and to ask that they remember not only the feasting but the days of fasting. I do not think I shall ever forget my fear during those three days when I was alone in my room. Nor shall I forget the sound of the shofar or walking through the seven gates, one by one.

I am over seventy now and my hair is white. Many people say I was very brave, but I do not remember feeling brave. I remember feeling afraid, yet, despite my fear, wishing to help my people.

From my window I watch the sky darken. I hear music and shouts of laughter. People are dancing in the streets, dressed in wild, funny costumes. Young children dress as grown-ups. Grown-ups dress as children. A jester is turning cartwheels. The laughter comes closer. Purim is about to begin.

I will walk into the courtyard garden. The guests will gather around to listen. I will slowly begin to speak the words of this story. Then when I tire, another person will continue the story. The story will pass from one to another. I think that is how it was meant to be. Once it was my story. Now it belongs to each of us.

Purim

King Ahasuerus has been linked with Xerxes I (486–465 B.C.E.), who ruled Persia and created the great city of Persepolis. According to oral legend, his son Darius II may have been Esther's child.

Whether the Book of Esther is historical fact, a legend, or a combination of both, Jews throughout the world continue to remember and celebrate the holiday of Purim in four ways: by eating and drinking, by giving food to friends, by giving gifts to the poor, and by reading the Book of Esther from the Megillah. In the synagogue, the Megillah, or scroll, is unrolled, but before it is read, it is folded in imitation of the letters that the Jews received from Mordecai and Esther.

Traditionally, Jews, both children and adults, also prepare for the holiday by creating playful skits, which are often embellished with the events of the day, and by making amusing and sometimes shocking masks and costumes to celebrate the time when their world was turned topsy-turvy.

Purim takes place each year for two nights at the time of the full moon during the month of Adar (February–March).

S-5/14   LU-10/07   3 circs   20/16